# Luella and Nita the Owl

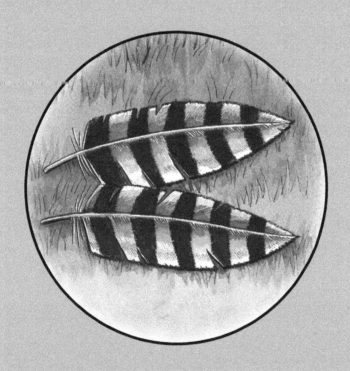

Written by Nancy Gaenzle
Illustrated by Paul Bush

Archway Publishing books may be ordered through booksellers or by contacting:

Archway Publishing
1663 Liberty Drive
Bloomington, IN 47403
www.archwaypublishing.com
1 (888) 242-5904

Because of the dynamic nature of the Internet, any web addresses or links contained in this book may have changed since publication and may no longer be valid. The views expressed in this work are solely those of the author and do not necessarily reflect the views of the publisher, and the publisher hereby disclaims any responsibility for them.

Any people depicted in stock imagery provided by Getty Images are models, and such images are being used for illustrative purposes only.
Certain stock imagery © Getty Images.

This is a work of fiction. All of the characters, names, incidents, organizations, and dialogue in this novel are either the products of the author's imagination or are used fictitiously.

ISBN: 978-1-4808-6322-4 (sc)
ISBN: 978-1-4808-6324-8 (hc)
ISBN: 978-1-4808-6323-1 (e)

Library of Congress Control Number: 2018946388

Print information available on the last page.

Archway Publishing rev. date: 6/1/2018

I dedicate this book to my mother,
# Waunita (Nita) Gaenzle.
Nita, you left this world before you had a chance to see your four girls grow into smart educated women. Teresa, Shirley, Jackie and I miss your love and laughter every day. I am proud of the title of this book, and I am proud to call you Mother.

The sun is just starting to peek over the windowsill in Luella's bedroom. Lu yawns and stretches and welcomes another beautiful summer day on the family farm.

As she looks out her bedroom window, she notices an owl landing on its perch high in a big, majestic cottonwood tree that grows in the backyard. The owl is returning home to her nest after an exhausting night of hunting food for her family.

Luella, still in her nightgown, watches from her window as this wise bird grooms her feathers. Luella can't help but notice that one of her tail feathers seems to droop just a bit.

Momma calls from the downstairs kitchen that breakfast is ready. Luella changes into her play clothes and rushes downstairs.

While eating her breakfast, Luella tells her mother about the owl that is living in the tree.

Momma explains to Luella how important it is not to disturb any mother animal who is caring for her young.

The mother owl reminds Luella of her Grandma Nita. When she comes to visit, she gives Luella such warm, loving hugs with outstretched arms, much like the wings of this owl. The name Nita would be perfect.

During breakfast, Momma informs Luella that the kind of owl living in the cottonwood tree is a great gray owl.

Momma next explains to Luella that owls have very unique eyes and necks. Their eyes do not move from side to side, but their necks can turn 270 degrees around. Momma encourages Luella to watch her new friend and see what else she can learn.

After Luella takes her dishes to the sink and thanks her momma for the yummy breakfast, she runs outside. She feels a very strong sense of responsibility to do everything she can to keep Nita the owl and her nest as safe as possible.

Luella pulls a chair near the base of the mighty cottonwood tree where she can see the owl's nest. She does not get too close because she does not want to make Nita the owl nervous.

Her new mission is to make sure everyone on the farm leaves Nita the owl and her nest alone.

One, two, ......three! There are three baby owlets popping their heads up from inside the nest. Oh, what a beautiful sight! This discovery makes Luella even more determined to protect her new feathery friends.

As the morning starts to unfold, the farm cat, Patches, meanders toward the shade of the tree. Luella scoops up Patches and takes her to the shade of the barn where she is soon distracted by a mouse running in the nearby grass.

Later, Ruby, Dad's ranch dog, walks over to Luella for a scratch behind the ears. Luella encourages Ruby to wander over and rest near the edge of the field where the cattle are grazing in the pasture.

Luella returns to the chair under the tree to discover her brother, John, is planning to climb the tree to make a tree house. She informs him that Nita the owl and her babies are now living in the tree. Everyone needs to be patient with this family until the babies are ready to fly.

Luella suggests to John that today would be an excellent day to ride his bike. The sun is out. The air is warm and inviting. He agrees and jumps on his bike for a journey of new discoveries that are waiting for him around the bend of the old dirt road.

Luella walks back to the tree and sits in the chair to rest. It has been a very busy morning.

The sun's warmth settles upon Lu like a cozy soft blanket. Soon she is fast asleep.

Several minutes pass before Luella opens her eyes. As she looks down at the ground to tie her shoelaces, she notices something special. Nita the owl has left her a present!

A beautiful tan and brown tail feather is resting next to her shoe.

Luella looks up at Nita the owl,
who is sitting beside her nest. As their
eyes meet, Nita gives Luella a big owl
wink. Luella can tell that Nita is very
pleased with her new friend.

Years have passed since
Luella and Nita first met.

Several generations of owls
have returned to raise their
baby owlets high in this majestic
cottonwood tree.

Even today, if you look closely, a feather or two can still be found.

# Coming Soon

*Luella's Christmas Surprise*

*Luella and Frank the Pheasant*

*Luella Visits Grandpa John's Cabin*

*Luella and Quincy the Quail*

*Luella and Mary the Mourning Dove*

**Nancy Gaenzle** was born and raised in a small town in southern Idaho on the Camas Prairie. Her love for wildlife comes from her grandmother, Mary Gaenzle, who had a special fondness for birds. Nancy, a retired schoolteacher, has one daughter, Marta, and one granddaughter, Luella. The Luella books are named after her granddaughter. The characters are named after actual family members to honor their legacy and their positive influence on her life.

**Paul Bush**, originally from Detroit, grew up in Idaho as child of two engineers. He, too, had his sights set on a career in engineering but decided calculus wasn't nearly as fun as drawing. Paul attended Utah State University, where he earned a bachelor's degree in Art, with an emphasis in Illustration. While Paul is new to illustrating children's storybooks, he has been creating illustrations and animations for the healthcare information industry for years, including education geared towards children. His work has been recognized and awarded in the industry.

Lightning Source UK Ltd.
Milton Keynes UK
UKHW050817090223
416624UK00003B/260